Autl

My name is Oliver Bowman and I am 14 years old. The Boy is my first published book. I have also written a screenplay about a lottery winner sharing his winnings amongst his split personalities, and I am busy writing my second book, which is a story told through the eyes of two dogs in World War 2, a German, and a Jewish dog.

I am publishing this book in memory of my cousin Emmie-Rose, who tragically passed away. All of the artwork in the book was created by Emmie. I am really proud that I've kept my promise to publish her artwork because she was an amazing artist. I hope that this book brings some comfort to her Mum, Dad and Roo.

I also want to thank Kate Major who helped edit my book, and my school

Beechwood, who continue to encourage my love of English and Drama.

My writing is inspired by my two heroes Ricky Gervais and Quentin Tarantino. My dream, one day, is to become a screenwriter and director. I would love to be as successful as my heroes.

I hope you enjoy reading The Boy.

Oli

Emmie-Rose Taylor

Emmie-Rose Taylor was a talented hand biro artist, who sadly left us at the tender age of 16. Em was a beautiful, kind girl who was always smiling. She will be missed by everyone who had the privilege to know her. Emmies dream was to be an illustrator...so there you are Emmie 'you made it!'

Table of Contents

The Boy Who Created a Religion

Words by Oli Bowman

Images by Emmie-Rose Taylor

Chapter One

The Lost Boy

Jerusalem, Police station, Police Officer Zeph

I thought it was going to be a normal day for me.

I would say goodbye to my wife and then go to the café to get breakfast, as her cooking has a bitter taste to it. In fact, walking into work was often my favourite part of the day, as everyone says good morning – the only attention someone like me would get.

"Morning Zeph, how are you?" they would say.

I would usually answer back with a joke, but not on this day.

Maybe that was a sign that it was not going

to be normal day; or, maybe it was just a coincidence?

My life had always been quite stable in Jerusalem. I lived with my wife in a two-bedroom apartment. I visited my mum and dad from time to time, but not often, as I never really had the time because my wife was pregnant. We had no pets because I felt there was no need to own them. They live, then they die like everything, I thought. My family was religious. My mum, my dad, and my wife. I had questions about God, but my questions never got answered, so I didn't ask them out loud. I knew people would just talk past my questions or be offended. I would have liked to have the same beliefs as my family and say I believed in God, but I didn't know how I could bring myself to with so many unanswered questions.

My Sergeant approached me. "I'm off as I've got something on, here are the keys to the station. I trust you know what to do?" His hand shook when he handed me the keys.

"Boss, are you ok?" I asked.

He didn't answer and just walked away. I

knew he had heard me, but he didn't react, and he didn't return.

12 o'clock arrived and I was the only one left at the station. I got changed from my uniform and was about to lock up, when I heard a sound. I slowly took out my gun and then I saw him, just a boy of about eight or nine years old.

He said these four simple words: "I just met God."

"What?" I asked.

"God. I met him."

I looked over at The Boy, his hands and face were covered in dirt, but his clothes were spotless. As I approached him, he said, "I can't see you, but I know you've moved. Do you want to know something?"

"Yes, umm, what do you mean you can't see?"

He stared straight through me and said calmly, "I'm blind, I was stuck in the desert for 66 days and nights and now I can't see."

My heart raced. "How did you get here then if you're blind?"

The Boy looked me in the eye and whispered, "you should probably put your gun away."

"But how do you know I have a gun if you're blind?"

He continued with no emotion. "You are wearing a pink shirt. Why have you changed clothes? Police don't normally wear their own clothing, do they?"

"Yes, they do," I said. "I'm on my way home."

Chillingly, he continued, "You live in a two-bedroom apartment with your pregnant wife, you hate her cooking, you think it's too bitter."

I paused. "Yes, how did you know?"

The Boy continued to speak calmly. "He told me, God."

I stared at The Boy as he sat down on a chair. I quickly picked up the phone and called my boss.

"Em Boss, I think you need to come back here now. I don't know how to explain this to you but I think I just met the Son of God."

Chapter Two

A Few Hours Before;
A Saved Life?

Jerusalem Outside the Police Station. Zeph's Commanding Officer Met the Boy

There were people everywhere outside the station – a huge gathering of people all approached The Boy. Everyone was mesmerized by the sight of him.

People shouted questions, left and right. "What is heaven like?" they asked. "What does God look like?"

The boy refused to answer and was just sitting there with his eyes shut! Practically everyone seemed to think that this boy was the most incredible thing they had ever seen; however, there are always people who are sceptical of mysterious situations such as this. Maybe they are right to be sceptical when there is no evidence to prove that God exists. (Well, at least there wasn't before!) Is the existence of this boy the evidence we have all been searching for?

Three men pushed past the crowd to get to The Boy and asked, "who do you think you are, misleading these people?"

"Just leave him alone," said someone from the crowd.

"WTF did you just say to me?" The man was furious and turned to him and punched him square in the nose. Blood squirted everywhere. A scuffle followed between the two men.

Then, The Boy stood up, opened his eyes and simply said "I'm hungry," with a deadpan voice. No one seemed to know what to say, but a few people offered him food. Then The Boy closed his eyes again and the two men who were fighting stopped.

I should have known at that moment that I would remember this day for the rest of my life.

12 hours had passed and people still gathered around The Boy showing just how far people's faith and patience will stretch when it comes to religion. Prayer mats were everywhere on the uncomfortable, dirty floor. Then The Boy opened his eyes again, but this time his eyes had changed. They had more colour, giving life to his personality, but somehow his emotions still did not show.

He pointed towards me and exclaimed, "Sergeant, you have cancer!"

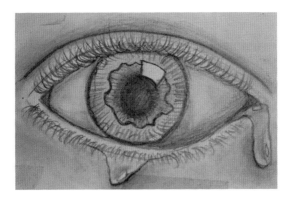

Everyone turned their heads.

I hadn't been feeling well lately, but I was just a little under the weather – nothing to worry about, I was sure. Had The Boy just saved my life? I started to walk away desperately trying to move through the crowd to get back to the station so I could give Zeph the keys and go home.

Chapter Three

The Boy and the Pope Meet

Italy, The Vatican, Leonardo Rossi Assistant to The Pope

Every day would start the same, with people lining up outside the Vatican to ask questions I could not answer – that were too impossible to answer. I believed in God, of course, otherwise why would I have chosen this life? But I always had hopes of becoming a doctor until I found God.

It was time to open the doors, but something was up. I was sitting on my chair for about an hour waiting for someone to show up, but no one came. I even went outside. I was shocked when I saw the front page of the newspaper, lying on the street: Messenger of God is in Israel.

I packed my things and got on the very next flight. I don't know why and I can't explain it, but I had to see this boy for myself.

Israel looked different from when I was last there many years ago. I walked towards the Western Wall of the Second Temple and saw a huge gathering of people. I asked one of the locals what was going on and he pointed to a circle of people praying and what looked like a sleeping boy, and standing over him was the Pope, our Pope, my boss. What was he doing here? He never leaves the Vatican! I approached him. Then I saw the most beautiful sight I have ever seen.

The Boy opened his eyes, glared at me, and then turned to the Pope and said, "You know who I am?"

"Yes I do, and you probably know who I am," said the Pope. "Apparently you have seen God, please tell me, what is he like?"

The Boy looked up. "No, not your God – the real God."

I interrupted their conversation. "What do you mean the real God?"

"The one that loves his people," said The Boy.

I was angered. How dare he speak about God that way? God loves everyone! I calmed myself, as I didn't want my words to hurt him – he was still only a child. I know religion creates freakish people who make up stories to get their voices heard. Maybe that's what was happening here?

The Pope looked shocked and sad and then walked away. I should have gone after him. Maybe The Boy was right and I wasn't thinking straight. I just let the Pope walk away from us and I just stayed where I was. I will regret that for the rest of my life because after that day, the Pope was never seen again.

People stopped believing in him and stopped visiting the Vatican. Others claim the Pope was killed, and others said he just gave up on life, gave up on God, and just wanted to disappear. But I knew that was far from the truth. I would not discover this, however, until it was too late. And me? Well, I found a new master…

Chapter Four

The Boy Becomes a Man (18 Years Old)

Five Years Later

Leonardo Rossi, the Boy's Disciple

The world has since transformed into something amazing: many diseases have been cured. I had to leave the Vatican and join The Boy. Everybody in the world now has faith in the afterlife and, everything in the world feels amazing, but nothing is ever perfect, is it?

However, there is a now a new disease that exists in the world. Only The Boy knows what this is or where it came from. If the world knew, the repercussions would be disastrous!

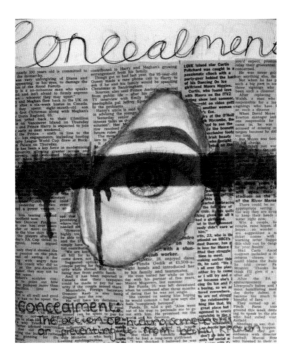

This disease has no known visual symptoms, but everyone who gets it eventually kill themselves. No one can know this, though, as it could result in a world without faith and a world without faith is a terrible place.

Now that the Pope had gone, The Boy was free to express his faith and a huge monument to commemorate his God had been built. Inside the monument is a vast room, a prayer chamber where The Boy spent most of his time.

The Boy is 18 years old now. His looks have completely changed. His nose is long and pointed; his cheeks are drawn making him look much more distinctive. His height has especially changed. Before, he was known to be short for his age, but now he is quite tall. I've followed him as his disciple now for many years. He is a man, but everyone still refers to him as The Boy.

"Hello. How's the situation?" The Boy asked as he walked through the doors of the monument.

"We have put them away next to you know who."

The Boy turned to me and nodded. He spoke quietly. "I'm going to pray to God now."

As I walked down the hall, I wonder how we can fix the situation. Inside the monument is a TARDIS-like structure – every time I cross the hall the look and feel of it changes. I would usually ignore information like this and concentrate on the important things, but for now, I can't help but worry about the small details. The Boy kneeled, he was quiet for a long time. I saw it in his face, I knew him well and I'm sure he heard God speak to him. He turned to me and said "I know what to do!"

Chapter Five

A New Disease

Drake, Scientist and New Believer

For some reason, no one was able to leave their homes. I mean, I loved spending time with my family, but not all the time, not every minute of every day. Ever since this new religion had been put into place, we all went by their rules.

We lived in Leeds, England. Our house was not so amazing, it was just a normal house that you would find anywhere in England. I lived with my wife and three boys, James, Adam, and Zack.

I was fortunate, though, as us scientists were instructed to meet in Rome. At least I would get a break from my four walls.

Just before I left, I took one more look at the house. I didn't like sharing my emotions much, mainly because of my upbringing. But I picked up my bag and got into the taxi and waved goodbye to my family. Of course, I knew they were not looking, but I just wanted God to know that I waved, that I cared.

The taxi driver was quite a character. He had long black hair down to his shoulders and huge glasses.

"Gum"? He asked.

"Oh I'm fine, thank you."

"So what brings you to the airport? He asked.

"Business," I said, trying to get him to stop talking to me.

"I'm Michael by the way, and you are Drake."

He kept talking to me for two hours until we finally got to the airport.

"Well, thank you how much do I owe you?" I asked.

"£100."

I nodded. "Here you go and may God bless you."

"May God bless you, too."

When I entered the airport, I found the prayer room and took out my mat and prayed to God. Now that things have changed, we celebrate God every day instead of just Christmas and Easter. We must pray for an hour every day and we must show God our respect by thanking him for sending us The Boy.

Four Hours Later:

Italy was beautiful and everywhere seemed so quiet and calm. We, the scientists, had to wear bright orange jumpsuits. It felt a bit weird that the streets were empty, but I was just happy to be in Italy. It was my first time inside the monument; we approached a huge door, then it opened and I saw him, something I've been waiting to see for years.

There he was, in front of me, The Boy.

"Shall we start?" he asked.

The Boy by Oli Bowman

Chapter Six

The World Starts to Die

Drake, Scientist and New Believer

The Boy sat us down and explained to us that the world was dying, and that he needed us.

Confused, Bill said, "what do you mean its dying? We can't do much with that, what are we supposed to do?"

"Follow me," said The Boy.

He led us to a room. "You have two choices: you can head back home and be with your family, or you can stay here and help and you will lead your family into the afterlife."

I glanced around the room. I wanted to

know what other people would do before I made my choice, but no one did anything. We were all strangely both scared and interested.

"Ok" he said.

He nudged the door open and I saw the most horrific thing I have ever seen in my life. It shocked me. I couldn't believe what I was seeing. A man had slit both his wrists and blood was trickling down his arms I couldn't stop looking at the blood. He had hung himself.

The boy just looked straight through me. "Follow me" he said.

Everyone left even Bill, everyone except me I couldn't move I just stared in shock.

Zeph Police Officer for the New Religion

I was walking past the room and I saw a man staring at what was left of Father Patterson. I tried to get the man's attention. He looked shocked.

"You wouldn't want to catch what he had; erm, my name's Zeph, by the way."

"I'm Drake, what do you mean?" Drake asked.

I just ignored his question and walked into the room and approached the body.

"Who is he? asked Drake.

Then something strange happened. I heard something, a voice in my head telling me to touch him. Drake and I stepped towards the body.

"What is this disease? asked Drake.

Something had caught my eye. There were scratch marks on the dead man's wrist.

I was about to touch the marks, as I couldn't help myself but then Bill said, "Zeph, Drake, come on he's going to explain what going on."

"This disease reveals something

devastating, something that makes me worried," said The Boy.

"What?" asked someone.

"What should we do?" asked Bill.

The Boy stared at us. "Don't tell anyone outside of these four walls, otherwise God will get mad. And don't touch anyone that has it."

"What should we do?" I asked The Boy.

"Sacrifice," he said.

Chapter Seven

Does He Speak from God or Not?

Leonardo Rossi, The Boy's Disciple

Luckily, this disease had only majorly affected one town so far, so we had to act fast and quarantine the town of Stoke. We felt helpless until we came up with an idea. We would isolate the town by building a dome around it; however, to build a dome big enough would take a long time, as Stoke was a big town. But I would be proven wrong – one day he led us to a room the size of a football pitch, and there it was a huge dome ready to be installed.

"How did you know?" I asked.

The Boy had no reaction he simply stared at the dome and said "God tells me the brilliance of others."

(The School in Stoke) Three Months Later:

The Schoolboy

My mates and I were messing around on the way to school today – a normal day for us, as we kicked over plants and threw stones at windows. That was pretty much the only fun we had. I lived with my brother and my mum in a bungalow. My mum worked at Tesco, so I found it quite easy to steal stuff. My brother sold the things I stole. He told mum he went to school, but really, he just hung outside selling food and he charged around £20 for each bag.

School for me was boring; I saw no purpose to going, and there was nothing I got out of it, apart from messing around with my friends. I enjoyed school that particular day mainly because my mate set poppers off in the classroom. I was laughing with my pals when the school bell went off and the teachers looked worried. They told us to leave the school slowly. We started walking outside thinking it was someone in six form setting the fire alarm off again. Then the teachers started screaming at us, telling us to run. We reached the gates of the school and then we saw it, this large object which looked about 1000 feet tall and about 8000 feet wide it was one of the most amazing and confusing things I have ever seen.

A man with a microphone spoke. "You are now in quarantine please do not attempt to leave, in God's name our seer has seen the future and we will get through this together; daily we will send supplies of food and water, this shouldn't be for long please look after each other and stay well in God's name."

In God's name, what does he mean in God's name?

We were all confused. Ok, I thought to myself, look on the bright side, the good thing is we had been let out of school early, but what the hell was going on? They said everything will be fine…EVERYTHING WILL BE FINE!?!

Chapter Eight

The Quiet Place

Drake, the Scientist and New Believer

Two months into the project and it was working. When I had the original idea, deep down I didn't think it would work, but I was amazed to find out it did. I was so proud of myself, but I tried not to show it in front of our Lord and Saviour. I just hoped that the whole thing would be over sooner rather than later. We were based in Italy and I was so far away from my family. I wanted to go home to see my family again because I had been away for so very long.

My thoughts were interrupted by The Boy's disciple.

"Everyone gather around!" he shouted.

The disciple was a large man. He wore a lab coat that was too small for him; and his voice was soft, deep, and strong.

I yawned. I was starting to feel a little tired, but the weird thing was I didn't know why. I mean I was working, but not too hard. It had only been a week since we originally put the dome up, so I should not have been as tired as I was. I found myself wondering again, not for the first time: could it be the water The Boy is giving us before we go to bed? No, it can't be, I am probably being paranoid?

The disciple's voice stopped my mind from wondering. "I'm sure you've noticed the success of our plan in containing Stoke, but we only really have two men to thank: Drake Harris and of course our seer, our God, The Boy. I'd like to reassure you all we will be visiting Stoke tomorrow so I'd like you to pack only the essentials needed, may God bless you."

May God bless you too," everybody replied.

Luckily, this time, we were able to fly. When we took the dome to Stoke, we had to travel by ship. The trip was jarring and very long but this time it only takes us three hours.

The problem with the disease was that no one was able to leave their houses other than for essentials like food, medical problems, or important meetings. But my happiness did not last long, because I never for one minute prepared myself for what I was about to see.

Everything was quiet. No one made a sound. Nothing. Not a single noise. Inside…everything just…blood…blood, everywhere. What happened? God promised didn't he that he would save everyone, but it isn't possible! How can they be dead? I looked at my colleague Bill and I fell to my knees at the sight of four young dead bodies all in school uniforms.

I couldn't sleep. I stayed up all night thinking about what could have happened. Was it my fault? Then I remembered that Bill wrote to his family! What if he had said something? They will blame me – it was my idea, my creation.

So, I opened the door to his room and stood there thinking, am I going to do this? I did not want to hurt Bill because he was my friend, but I knew that God wanted this. I can't explain how I knew, but the voices in my head were telling me to do this.

Quietly I took the pillow from the bed next to him and pushed it hard on his face. "Stop…. stop!" screamed Bill in a muffled voice. He kicked back hard, but I pushed down harder and harder with all my strength until he stopped moving.

Chapter Nine

Who Knows?

Adam, Scientist; Drake's Roommate

We were all awoken from our sleep and rushed into what seemed to be a panic room, which I was quite happy about as I really needed to take my mind off of Drake. I was worried about him and angry with him. He always left our room in such a mess, and I wanted to speak to him about it, but he had disappeared. To be honest, though, the main question I kept asking myself was: why did they have a panic room in the first place??

"Gentleman I have brought you here, as sadly Bill Marsh has died, news of the death won't be released. One by one you will be questioned about this starting with

Adam."

I walked over quite scared, there was a lot going on there that I didn't know about. Bill was dead and Drake was gone? But I didn't want anyone knowing how I was feeling in case they thought I had something to do with it, so I held my head up high.

He led me to a room which was bright white. Even the table and the chair were white, and they were the only accessories in the room. There was a man holding a notepad and pencil.

"Hello sir," he said. "I just want to ask a couple questions."

"Sure," I said. I really wanted to ask about Bill, but I needed to play it cool. That's what my wife said, she used to tell me that I always asked too many questions, I always got myself involved in things that I shouldn't have.

"Do you know Drake Joshua at all?"

"Umm, well I've only known him for a short time. He is my roommate. Well, he *was*," I said. "What is it he's meant to have done?"

The man looked at me suspiciously. "Can I ask you, why did you say Drake 'was' your roommate?"

There I went again saying too much. I sputtered. "I mean he *is* my roommate but I've not seen him today."

The man stared at me angrily. "He has upset God!"

"What do you mean upset God" I asked.

The man stood up from his chair and walked around to where I sat. He stood right next to me and stared down at me and said, "he's taken God's love and corrupted it with his evil."

Ten more minutes followed of me being bombarded with questions that I couldn't and didn't answer. Then I had to sit and wait another hour while others were questioned until I heard a voice shouting "Drake…Drake is escaping to England!"

No one reacted. No one could hear it but me, the voice was in my head the voice seemed upset, like it had been crying but a strange happy cry, tears of happiness.

"Who are you?" I asked.

Then I heard footsteps followed by a light, a bright light that shone over a man standing naked with axe wounds all over his arms.

"I saw it I saw it all!" he screamed at me.

I jumped from my seat everybody looked at me. Was it a dream? Had I fallen asleep? I hoped it was. I looked up to find the same man who had been questioning us in the white room telling us all that the questioning had finished, and we could all return to our rooms to get some sleep.

How can I sleep? I was scared to sleep ever again.

Chapter Ten

The State of the World

Tim, Head of the National Suicide Service

My name is Tim and I am the head of the NSS National Suicide Service. I haven't always worked in this field; in fact, I used to be a surgeon. But, not anymore. All major illnesses, like cancer, are no longer a problem. Sure, some people have the occasional broken bone, but nowadays people aren't really into dangerous sports like climbing trees and jumping out of planes. All sports are non-contact, so people never usually get hurt. In a way, there is really no need for people like me anymore, or the police because there is no more crime. The new religion says the only way to go to Heaven is to live a peaceful quiet simple life.

Here in Columbia no one can live outside these rules. You can no longer be gay, everyone is the same, no one stands out, everyone eats a simple diet of grass and milk. I cannot say it is all good, but it seems to make people happy – well, most people. And that's why I'm needed and why I oversee the NSS.

Until I found this job, I used to go to the job centre to try and find something, or I made money by hosting my house as a prayer lair, which makes more money than you think. I live in the centre of Colombia with my wife and our two children. We have always wanted to transfer to England, but now my job is too important here to move. I stand on the streets for 12 hours every day until my shift is swapped and then I can return home.

I had already been standing on the streets for six hours and nothing had happened! Everyday I'm expected to spot people who have signs that just maybe they are thinking about killing themselves, but I rarely have anything to report, so work here is kind of laid back but the rest of the world is not as fortunate as us. The NSS in England, that's where I would really like to work, they have to wear full body suits, and no one can leave their house especially in a town called Stoke where the disease is terrible.

My shift was over and I was walking home which was normally insanely dark by 9 pm. No one had a light on in their house, so much so that I brought a flashlight wherever I went. But today every light, every single light remained on. It freaked me out a little, so I decided to run home rather than walk and when I reached my house, I saw my wife and children holding the newspaper.

"What's happened?" I asked.

"They have found it." My wife said.

I stared at her. "You mean the cure? Have they found the cure?"

Chapter Eleven

Part One: Two Hours Before the End!

Adam, Scientist; Drake's Roommate

It was hours ahead of the time we usually finish up in the research lab, but now it was far more important than ever to keep going. The death rate had just reached its first thousand and the only way to contain it, was to destroy it before it spread.

"I'm going to head out now. I'm going to return to my room" said my colleague Gary. "I think I'm going to work more with this rabbit, surely there is a cure, I don't know why but I have to keep going."

"Ok I'll see you in our room," I replied.

Gary was concerned. He looked as if he was worried about me.

I couldn't leave the lab yet; the disease was getting worse every day and so were my nightmares – they had become too much ever since the interview. Ever since Drake had disappeared, I kept on seeing him in my mind. It's probably nothing, but something seemed very wrong.

I inserted the virus into the main vein of the rabbit. I was wearing my safety gloves of course. The whole lab was safety-proof, but for these experiments using animals we had to be really careful. Just a single drop of the virus could have made you go mad, made you kill yourself. I was expecting the same result as all the other animals we tested, mice, hamsters, cats, dogs, their lungs would collapse, so of course I had to step back ready for an explosion of sorts. I took cover behind the lab screen and I tightened the grip to my ears getting ready to hear something. But no…nothing not a single sound. I looked to see if the rabbit was still breathing. It was!

I went screaming down the hall shouting that I had found the cure and waking everyone. I walked into my room to find

The Boy, who was standing there.

He had no expression on his face. "Good job, God told me that it would be you who would find the cure, I wonder would you like to have dinner with me?"

I was confused, I had just told him I found the cure and he's asking me to dinner?!? A strange reaction but…I could never refuse the messenger of God.

The cure was spread around every corner of the world to be mass produced by every

nation individually. The cure was just grass that's why Colombia had not been infected, as almost everyone there had taken up the diet of grass. Now I could relax and it was time for my reward, dinner with The Boy.

Chapter Eleven

Part Two: The Resurrection

Dinner time: It was the first time I had ever entered the place of God on my own. He sat at a huge table with just two chairs on either side, so I took my seat.

As usual with him, it was my place to start the conversation.

"So this place is lovely."

"It's God's place and only the people of God our allowed here." He said.

"I'd like to thank you for giving the scientists like me a chance to find the cure. This is the reason I'm alive and my family is alive there's only one thing to say and that is thank you."

The Boy nodded at me and smiled.

"Adam I'd like to show you something." He got off his chair and lead me to a doorway.

"You have a choice Adam. You can enter, or you can leave and never come back."

I didn't know what he meant, but I also didn't want to miss out on anything; no one gets to eat on their own with The Boy. I didn't hesitate in my response.

"Yeah I want to go" I answered.

I opened the door. The hallway was dark and there was nothing but blackness. I couldn't hear or even see The Boy. Then I saw a light. I had nowhere else to walk so I carried on straight ahead. There was a huge TV screen and the screen was blank. Then, suddenly, it wasn't. I was confused. There was footage of people – horrific footage of people being attacked and murdered. Amongst the footage, I recognised the people, my colleagues, all the scientists. They were all being suffocated by a shadowy figure.

I panicked. I was in darkness and I couldn't see The Boy. Where was he?

"Hello!!" I yelled. "Is anyone there?" A door suddenly opened I walked inside.

"Master? Boy??" I yelled.

Then I heard a scream. It was The Boy.

"I'm not a boy, my name is Oliver Graham," he said. I heard the voice scream all around me. "I'm far from a boy and I'm fed up of people calling me that!"

Then the lights flashed on and I saw someone. It was Drake! But he was eating something and there was blood soaking around his mouth his skin frail and grey. He turned to me and simply said, "this is God punishing us."

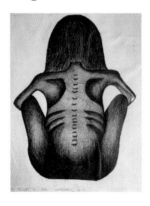

"Here, let's share" said Drake. Something rolled towards me. To my horror, it was a head.

Drake was muttering to himself. He had lost his mind. "It was only a few weeks ago we tried to save the world didn't we? It was our job, we did what he told us to, we had no choice because our God told us we had to do anything to save everyone…it wasn't my fault!!"

What had happened to Drake? Had he gone mad? I wondered.

I screamed my loudest trying to appeal to The Boy, telling him I understood he was a man not a boy, but he didn't listen to me. All I could hear was him muttering to himself: "we all must die! we all must die!"

I looked down at my feet. There was a body, and beside it a piece of paper. A body, a headless body of a man in religious robes. It was the Pope! I screamed, grabbed the paper, and ran out of the room. I slammed the door. I needed to lock it quickly! I panicked and my hands shook, but after what seemed like a hundred times of trying I locked it and slid to the floor looking at the piece of paper in my hand.

What I saw shocked me, I couldn't believe my eyes, it was a medical paper and this would be the last thing I saw!

I screamed. "The Boy Oliver, he was no God, he was a psycho!"

The End

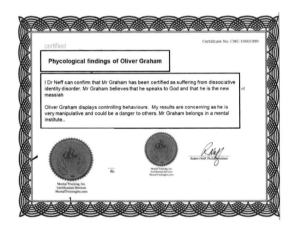

Printed in Great Britain
by Amazon